Hans Wilhelm

Little Whale in Deep Trouble

A story inspired by a true event

BARRON'S

Oscar and his mother
live in the deep waters of
the big ocean.

They are always together.

Oscar loves his home. Animals of all
colors, sizes, and shapes swim around them.

He always feels safe when he sees the two
huge shadows gliding below him on the ocean
floor.

The bigger one is his Mama's shadow
and the smaller one is his.

Every now and then Oscar and Mama
Whale rise to the surface of the ocean for air.

Oscar's Mama blows a huge fountain
of water through her blowhole.

Oscar tries very hard. But his
water fountain is much
smaller.

Sometimes they stay on the surface and play.

They jump up and flip backward. Mama makes a big splash.

Oscar makes the best splash he can.

Then they dive down again.

One day, a school of stingrays comes cruising by.

Oscar wonders where they are going.

Before he knows it, he is swimming
after the stingrays.

He has not gone far when he looks down.

Uh, oh!

There is only one shadow beneath him
—his own.

Where is his Mama?

Oscar quickly turns around to look for his mother—

but suddenly he can't move his flippers.

He can't swim!

He is caught in a fishing net.

Oscar tries to shake the net off.

But the more he tries the tighter the ropes of the net wrap around him.

Oscar is in deep trouble!

He knows that soon he must get up to the surface to breathe.

If only his Mama were here to help him. If only he had not followed the stingrays.

Luckily, Oscar can wiggle his tail.

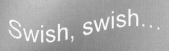

Swish, swish...

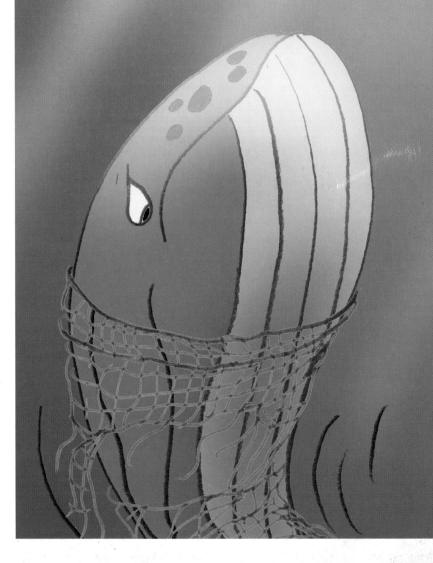

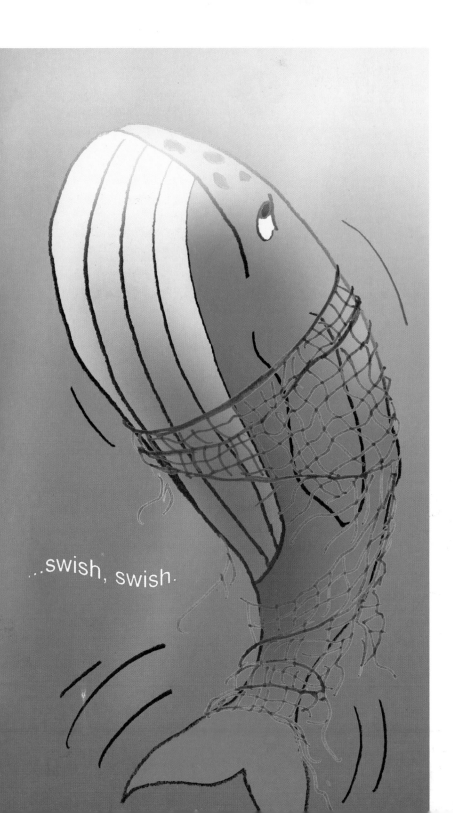

...swish, swish.

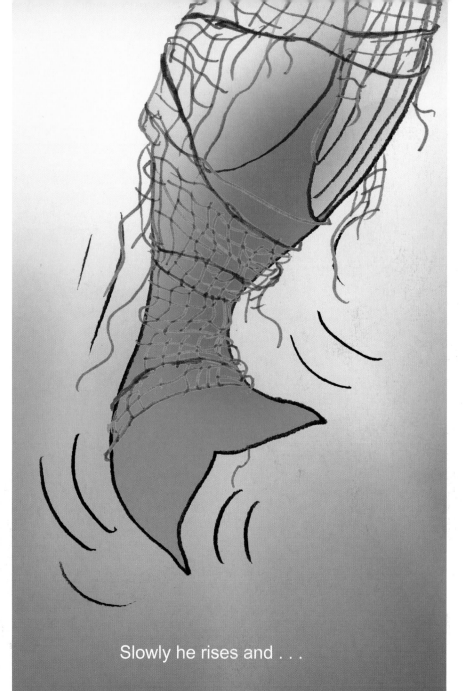

Slowly he rises and . . .

. . . at last he is up to the surface.

He takes in a deep breath of air.

Oscar does not know it, but some people see his water fountain.

And they also notice the fishing net wrapped around his body.

Soon two very strange creatures
come swimming toward Oscar.

He sees their flippers. Could they be
some strange kind of fish? he wonders.

But he had never seen such fish before.

One of the divers comes very close. Oscar is afraid.

He wants to swim away. But he can't.

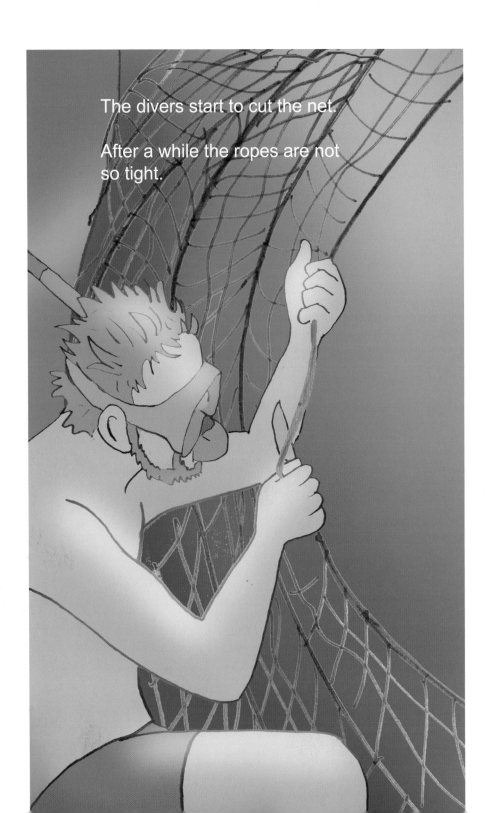

The divers start to cut the net.

After a while the ropes are not so tight.

Oscar is not afraid anymore.

Somehow he knows these creatures have come to help him.

Bit by bit the net falls away.

One flipper,

two flippers . . .

Finally the last piece of netting
is cut off his tail and . . . .

....Oscar is free!

The strange creatures have
rescued him!

Oscar is so happy that he
swims around and around,
and then . . . .

. . . he does a THANK YOU dance.

He jumps up and flips over backward in the waves.

THANK YOU!

THANK YOU!

He does it over and over again, clapping his flippers and waving his tail.

THANK YOU!

When Oscar dives back into the water
he has a wonderful surprise—his Mama
is waiting for him!

She had been searching for him everywhere.
When she heard the splashing and crashing
she knew just where to find her little Oscar.

Now they are together again, and so are their two shadows, gliding across the ocean floor.

HUMPBACK WHALE

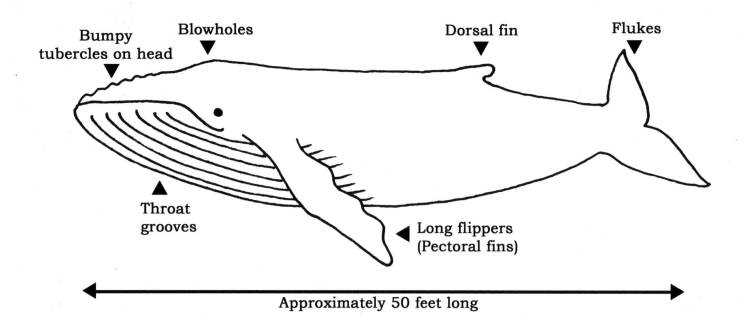

Bumpy tubercles on head ▼

Blowholes ▼

Dorsal fin ▼

Flukes ▼

Throat grooves ▲

Long flippers (Pectoral fins) ◀

◀ Approximately 50 feet long ▶

In the winter of 2011, some friends went out on their boat for whale watching off the Pacific coast of Mexico. Coming across a young humpback whale caught in a fishing net they decided to rescue the whale. Once freed, the whale thanked them with an amazing dance.

It is estimated that over 300,000 whales and dolphins are caught every year in ropes, nets, and fishing lines. Courageous people have freed many of them from their boats or by approaching these giants with snorkels or scuba gear. Their incredible rescue operations have inspired this story.

Every year countless marine animals also suffer from the trash that we throw away. Some of our garbage floats into the open sea where animals mistake it for food or get caught with their neck or body in items of plastic. It is our responsibility to keep our lands, rivers, and oceans clean so that nobody gets hurt.

Oscar and his mother are humpback whales. With their fins and tails they look like huge fish. But they are mammals. They have to breathe air—which they do through their blowholes on top of their bodies.

Humpback whales live in oceans around the world and can be seen near coastlines where they feed on plankton, tiny shrimp-like krill, and small fish. They can eat up to a ton of food a day.

They are powerful swimmers and can leap out of water and slap the water with their flukes (tail) and pectoral fins. It is a spectacular sight that attracts whale watchers all over the world.

Humpback whales are also known for their magical songs. These songs vary greatly and can go on for hours.

Every year humpback whales migrate from summer-feeding grounds near the poles to their winter-feeding grounds in warmer waters around the equator.

There used to be a large number of humpback whales in our oceans. But for many years people have hunted these beautiful giants. Their number has been dwindling substantially and today they are among the most endangered whales.

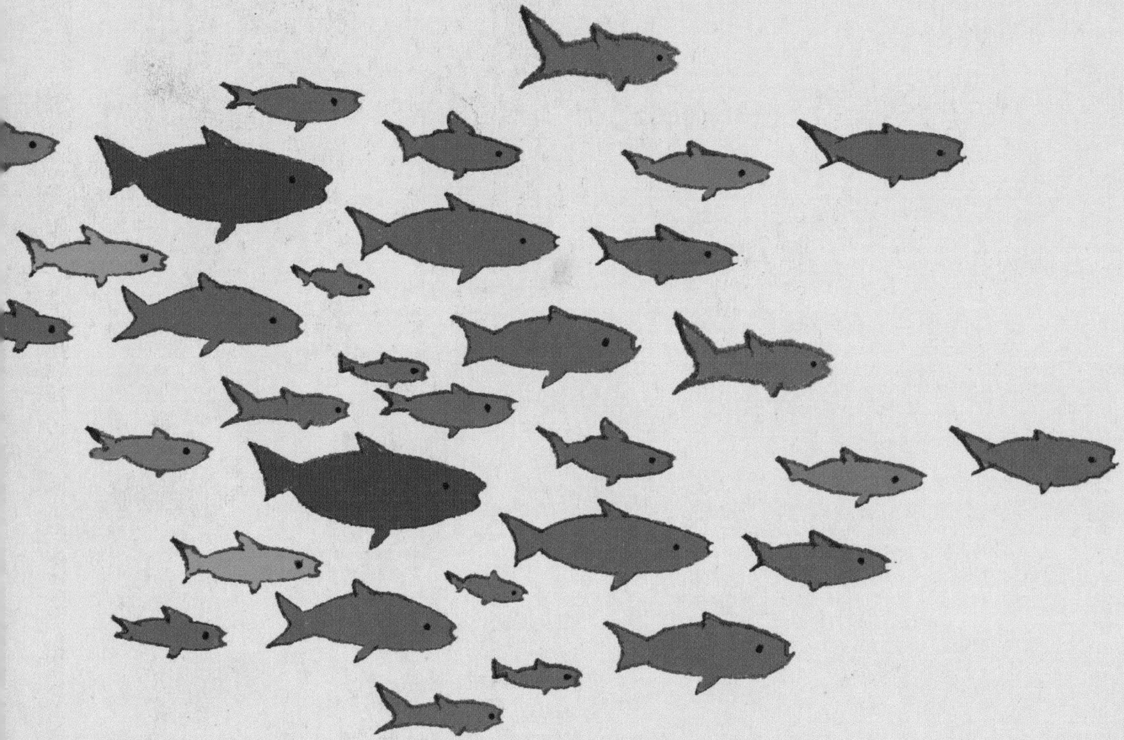